This book
belongs to

....

Puddle's Fan Pages

Here's what other children have to say about their favourite puppy and his latest adventure!

"Puddle is really funny because when they were swinging the lasso he jumped up and caught it and started swinging it around. I like Puddle as a character because he's funny and naughty and gets into mischief." Layla, age 8

"This was a very very very good book. I really like the Puddle books. " Saara, age 7

"I liked the bit where they all fell down, it made me laugh." Abby, age 6

"The funniest bit is when a cowboy hat lands on top of Puddle and he can't see and causes chaos in the corral. The kids have cool nicknames like Rodeo Ruby and Hawkeye Harry, and get to ride on ponies and horses." Madeleine, age 6

"Yee haw!! Cowboy School Rocks!"
Piper, age 7

"I love it. It was great. My favourite
bit was when they chased Outlaw Pete.
I liked Lil." Caitlin, age 7

"I liked Little Lil and Tumbleweed the
best. Tumbleweed is a clever pony
because he carried Ruby and Harry and
Lil on his back. Little Lil says funny things
like 'Ding, dang, dong'. She's really funny!"
Maia, age 5

Star of the School

Puddle
the naughtiest puppy

Star of the School

by Hayley Daze
illustrated by David Opie
cover illustrated by Paul Hardman

A catalogue record for this book is available from the British Library

Published by Ladybird Books Ltd
A Penguin Company
Penguin Books Ltd., 80 Strand, London WC2R 0RL, UK
Penguin Books Australia Ltd., Camberwell, Victoria, Australia
Penguin Group (NZ) 67 Apollo Drive, Rosedale,
North Shore 0632, New Zealand

001 –

1 3 5 7 9 10 8 6 4 2

Series created by Working Partners Limited, London WC1X 9HH
Text © Working Partners Ltd MMXI
Cover illustration © Working Partners Ltd MMXI
Interior illustrations © Ladybird Books Ltd MMXI

Special thanks to Jane Clarke

ISBN: 978-1-40930-406-7
Printed in England

Mixed Sources

Product group from well-managed
forests and other controlled sources
www.fsc.org   Cert no. SA-COC-001592
© 1996 Forest Stewardship Council

FSC

For Caitlin, a Puddle super-fan!

When clouds fill the sky and rain starts to fall,
Ruby and Harry are not sad at all.
They know that when puddles appear on the ground,
A magical puppy will soon be around!

Puddle's his name, and he's the one
Who can lead you to worlds of adventure and fun!
He may be quite naughty, but he's clever too,
So come follow Puddle – he's waiting for you!

A present from Puddle:

Look out for the special code at the back of the book to get extra-special games and loads of free stuff at Puddle's website! Come and play at www.puddlethepuppy.com

Contents

Chapter One
Rodeo Ruby

"Come on, Hawkeye Harry!" Ruby cried, cradling a bulging pink water balloon in her hands. "Let's see if you're as quick on the draw as Rodeo Ruby!"

It was a boiling hot day, and Ruby and her cousin Harry

were in the garden behind Grandad's cottage. Harry was struggling to tie a knot in the top of his plump green water balloon. He looked at Ruby over the top of his glasses.

"In the Wild West," Harry said, "a shootout starts with the cowboys standing back to back. I read it in a book. They step nine paces away from each other, then on the tenth step, they turn and fire."

"Showdown time!" Ruby declared, standing with her back to Harry's.

"One, two, three…" The two cousins paced away from each other, counting in unison. "Eight, nine… TEN!"

They turned and threw the water
balloons at each other.

Splat! The pink balloon came down

on Harry's bare legs.

Splosh! The green balloon burst on Ruby's head.

"Rodeo Ruby has the fastest balloon in the West!" Ruby spluttered, shaking her damp plaits. The shower of water felt lovely and fresh.

"Hawkeye Harry hits the target better." Harry grinned as he polished his glasses on his T-shirt. "That was a bull's-eye!"

"Refill!" Ruby giggled. She took a handful of empty balloons out of her pocket, chose a blue one, and pulled its rubbery neck over the spout on Grandad's huge watering can. She held on to it as Harry tipped up the heavy metal can. Soon the blue water balloon was fat and wobbly. Ruby

pulled it off the spout and tied it.
They filled more and more balloons,
until the watering can was empty.

"Let the shootout begin!" Ruby
announced. They turned back to
back, counted ten steps, and then they
turned and hurled the water balloons
at each other.

Splat! Splosh! Splat! Splat! Splat!

21

Soon Ruby and Harry were soaked through and laughing so much it was hard to stand.

"We've made puddles all over the path," Ruby gurgled. "Grandad will think it's been raining!"

Plip! A ring appeared in one of the puddles. *Plip! Plip!*

There was a roll of thunder in the distance.

Ruby looked at Harry.

"It is raining!" She squealed in delight as warm raindrops plopped down around them. Whenever it rained, their naughty puppy friend Puddle appeared, and they went on magical adventures together.

"Woof! Woof!" A bark echoed from inside Grandad's empty watering can, and a cheeky little furry head popped out.

"Puddle! How did you get in there?"
Ruby pulled out the little puppy and
set him down next to her on the path.
Puddle's tail wagged and wagged.

Then he ran to the biggest puddle on the path, looked over his shoulder at Ruby and Harry . . . and jumped in. There was a big splash as he disappeared.

Ruby and Harry grinned at each other, and in they jumped, too.

Chapter Two
The Wild West

Ruby tugged on her plaits for luck
and slowly opened her eyes. They
were standing in a dusty street,
outside a row of wooden buildings.
A stagecoach was trundling slowly
up the road on wooden wagon
wheels. Right next to them, a horse
was tied to a rail under a sign that
read: SALOON. A man wearing a

cowboy hat and boots entered the
building. The double doors swung
shut behind him.

"Wow! We're in the Wild West,"
Harry gasped. "Look – there's even
a WANTED poster stuck on the
saloon door!"

WANTED

Outlaw Pete for
Livestock Rustling!

Ruby ran up to it.
The poster showed
a picture of a mean-
looking cowboy with
a spotted bandana
tied round his neck.

Ruby read the poster aloud.
"WANTED – Outlaw Pete for
Livestock Rustling!"

"That means stealing animals,"
Harry explained.

Ruby whirled around. "Where's
Puddle?" she asked. "Has he been
rustled by Outlaw Pete?"

"Outlaws don't rustle puppies,
they rustle cows and horses," Harry
chuckled. He pointed up the dusty

street. "There's Puddle. He's running up to those three cowboy children!"

Ruby and Harry raced to catch up with their little puppy friend. Ahead of them, two young cowboys were standing on either side of a very small cowgirl. The two boys were swinging long ropes with loops tied at the end.

"This town ain't BIG enough for the three of us!" one of the boys yelled at the little cowgirl. He whirled his looped rope around his head. The other boy did the same. "Those two big cowboys are picking on that little cowgirl," Ruby panted as they ran towards the cowboy kids.

"They're trying to lasso her," Harry puffed. "It's how cowboys catch cattle and horses."

"Hey! Stop being mean!" Ruby shouted, grabbing at one of the boys' ropes. Her fingers closed on empty air, but to her relief, the tiny cowgirl managed to dodge out of the way.

The other boy whirled his lasso. Harry leapt up and tried to snatch hold of it, but the rope was moving too fast to catch. The boys made

their ropes snap
and whizz through
the air like bolts
of lightning.

"Yip! Yip! Yip!"
Puddle yapped excitedly as Ruby
and Harry tried again and again to
grab the ropes.

"Puddle, it's not a game!" Harry
yelled as the naughty little puppy
hurled himself into the air.

Snap! Puddle's teeth closed round
the loop of one
of the lassos. The
boy who had been
waving it hung on
to the other end

and tried to shake the puppy off.

"*Grrr!*" Puddle growled, clamping the lasso firmly between his jaws.

"Get off, little doggie!" the boy shouted. The other boy dropped his lasso and ran to help.

There was a muffled "Woof!" and Puddle began to race round and round the two boys, holding the lasso in his mouth.

"That's it, Puddle! Tie them up!" Ruby cheered as Puddle wound the coils of rope around the boys' legs.

Whump!

The trussed-up boys fell over in a heap in the dust.

Ruby, Harry, Puddle and the tiny cowgirl watched as the boys rolled around, trying to untangle the rope.

The boys struggled to their feet.

"We'll be back!" they muttered as they sloped off with their lassos in knots.

"Gee, thanks!" the little cowgirl exclaimed. She was wearing a normal-size cowboy hat, but it was so large on her that it fell down over her eyes. She patted Puddle on the head. "What's your name, little partner?" she asked.

"That's our puppy, Puddle," Ruby said proudly. "I'm Rodeo Ruby and this is my cousin, Hawkeye Harry."

"Howdy, strangers!" The little cowgirl raised her hat, revealing her freckled face and a pair of bright red bunches. "Welcome to the town of Wagging Tail. My name's Lil." She grinned, showing the gap between her teeth. "Everyone calls me Lil the Littlest Cowgirl."

"Who were those two nasty boys?" Ruby asked.

"My twin big brothers, Hank and Walt." Lil sighed. "They're not always mean, but Cowboy Clint is holding auditions for Cowboy School at noon today, and Hank and Walt say I'm way too small to take part."

"That's not fair!" Ruby said.

"Woof!" Puddle sounded as if he agreed.

"Puddle knows what it's like to be tiny, too," Lil murmured, stroking his ears.

"Don't worry, Little Lil," Ruby told their new friend. "Rodeo Ruby and Hawkeye Harry will figure something out!"

Chapter Three
Down on Four Paw Ranch

"I've read about how you can make yourself look taller," Harry said. "Maybe Lil could wear a bigger hat . . ."

Lil looked at him from under her huge hat. "That's plum crazy," she said. "This one's big enough."

"Maybe we could make your boots higher. We could strap blocks of wood to the bottom of them, like stilts," Harry suggested.

"I'd have to get some long jeans to cover them up," Lil replied, "and even then, I'd still be real short. There's just not enough of little old me," she said sadly.

Ruby put her hands on her hips and tilted her head. She looked first at Lil and then at Harry.

"I've got an idea!" she exclaimed. "Where can we get some grown-up clothes?"

"Back at the ranch," Lil said, perking up. "Follow me!"

Lil dived through an arched gateway with a sign that read:

WELCOME TO FOUR PAW
RANCH. She raced up a dusty path
to a rickety old wooden farmhouse.

A sturdy piebald pony looked up from the bag of oats he was munching and whinnied a greeting.

"That's my pony, Tumbleweed," Lil proudly told Ruby and Harry.

She stuck her head indoors.

"Cooo-eee!" she called.

There was no reply.

"We're in luck! Ma and Pa are out," Lil said, leading the way through

the hall. She pushed open the doors
of her parents' bedroom. There was
a big yellow jacket, with tassels all
down the sleeves, lying on the bed.

"This is just what we need," Ruby
said, holding up the jacket and
making the tassels flap. "Lil, can you
sit on Harry's shoulders?" she asked.

"Sure thing, Rodeo Ruby," Lil
said.

She jumped on to the bed while
Harry bent down beside it. Lil
clambered on to Harry's shoulders.
Harry grabbed her ankles and
carefully stood up.

"Well done – this is going to
work," Ruby said. She climbed on to

a chair so she could help Lil into the
yellow jacket. It was so big that it fell
down over Harry's head and body.
Only his legs stuck out.

"You need some boots." Ruby
looked round the room. Next to the
door was a pair
of sturdy brown
leather cowboy
boots with spiky
little metal wheels
on the heels.

They jangled as she helped Harry
step into the boots.

"Wow! These boots have got spurs
on them," said Harry's muffled voice
from inside the jacket.

Ruby stood back and clapped her
hands.

"Perfect!" she said. "Lil's a tall
cowgirl now."

Lil looked in the mirror. "Sure am," she said with a laugh.

Puddle sat down and scratched his ear with his back foot as he gazed at the strange sight in front of him.

"It's only Harry and Lil," Ruby reassured Puddle. "What should we call them? How about Cowboy Hil!"

"Or Cowgirl Lirry!" Lil giggled.

Puddle got up and wagged his tail as Ruby helped Harry and Lil out of the bedroom.

Slowly, they tottered out of the

ranch and down the main street, with
Ruby holding on to Harry's hand
and Puddle scampering behind.

"I can hear wagon wheels, but I can't see a thing!" Harry grumbled. "I'm Hawkeye Harry – I'm supposed to be able to see everything!"

"It's only a hay wagon," Ruby told him. "How far have we got to go?" she asked Lil.

"Cowboy School isn't far," Lil said. "Harry, I'll tell you when to turn."

A dappled-grey horse galloped past them in a cloud of dust.

"Woof!" Puddle barked in surprise.

Ruby caught a glimpse of the rider, who was wearing a spotted bandana.

"Why does he look familiar?" she murmured.

But Ruby didn't have time to
think about it. The dappled-grey
horse was running headfirst towards
a team of six big brown horses
pulling a heavy stagecoach down
the road behind them.

Just in time, the team of brown horses reared up and swerved out of the way as the dappled-grey horse charged past. But the brown horses had been startled, and their eyes

were wide with fear. The stagecoach they were pulling rocked wildly as they bolted.

Puddle yelped in alarm.

"The stagecoach is heading straight towards us!" Ruby yelled.

Chapter Four
Learning to Lasso

"Get out of the way! Quick!" Ruby grabbed the tassels on Lil's sleeve, pulling her and Harry aside. Her plaits flew into her face, and Lil's hat blew off as the stagecoach and horses thundered past in a rush of dusty wind. Puddle scooted out of the way with his tail between his legs.

"Phew!" Ruby breathed a sigh

of relief. But pulling on Lil's sleeve had made Lil wobble. Harry was tottering about, with Lil clutching on to him as if she were trying to ride a bucking pony. But it was no use. Lil lost her balance and . . .

"I'll catch you!" Ruby held up her arms as Lil toppled from Harry's shoulders. The big yellow jacket Lil was wearing wrapped itself round Ruby's head, and she and Lil fell in a heap, tripping up Harry, who landed smack on top of them.

"Yip! Yip! Yip!" Puddle yapped, jumping up and down.

There was a shout of laughter from across the road. It was Hank and

Walt. The only way Ruby could tell the twins apart was that one had H on his hat, and the other had W.

"Now who's all tangled up?" Hank chortled.

"It's Lil, the silliest cowgirl!" Walt sniggered. "If you think you can do the audition on someone's shoulders, you're crazier than a crazy coyote!"

Lil's big twin brothers walked off, laughing.

Lil picked up her hat. "Hank and Walt are right," she sighed. "We can't make me any taller. Maybe I should give up."

"Never!" Ruby said. "Not while Rodeo Ruby and Hawkeye Harry are here! We can help Little Lil impress Cowboy Clint with her cowgirl skills, can't we, Harry?"

"Sure can!" Harry declared in a fake Wild West accent. "I've read lots about lassoing," he said in his normal voice. "Let's go back to Four Paw Ranch and practise."

Lil dusted off her hat and plonked it back on her bunches. "All right!" she agreed, leading the way back to the ranch.

Tumbleweed looked up from the water trough at the side of the path as Lil fetched a lasso from her father's shed. "Try to lasso the gatepost," Ruby suggested.

Lil grabbed the rope in both hands and twirled it around, then let go of the end. The lasso snaked along at knee level and whizzed past Puddle's nose.

"Woof!" he barked in alarm.

Harry pushed his glasses up his nose. "The book said it's all about aerodynamics," he explained, taking the rope. "That means how air moves. You have to whirl the lasso around your head with one hand, then flick your wrist as you let go to give it power."

Harry flicked the length of rope so hard it made a cracking sound, like a whip.

"Let me have a go," Lil said, taking hold of the rope.

Soon Lil was lassoing the gatepost, then Tumbleweed, then Harry, then Ruby.

"You're brilliant at this!" Ruby told Lil as she stepped out of Lil's lasso. "Think you can lasso a little target?" She pointed to Puddle.

"Easy as pie!" Lil expertly whirled the lasso round her head. Puddle skittered about excitedly, trying to catch the rope.

The lasso whizzed through the air and looped gently round Puddle's body, bringing him to a halt.

"Yip! Yip! Yip!" Puddle barked, nipping at the rope.

"Wow!" Ruby gasped in admiration.

"If you show that much skill at the audition, Cowboy Clint's sure to let you into his school!"

"It must be nearly noon," Harry told them. "The sun's high in the sky and our shadows are very short."

"Then let's get going!" Ruby cried. "It's audition time!"

Chapter Five
Trouble at
Cowboy School Corral

Ruby, Harry and Puddle raced down
the main street after Lil. She swerved
under a wooden archway that had
COWBOY SCHOOL written in
shaky letters across the top.

"Down here!" Lil told them,
running along a narrow lane with
sheds and stables on either side.

They skidded to a halt in front of

a wooden enclosure full of beautiful
chestnut horses that neighed and
tossed their heads.

"The horses in this corral are really valuable," Lil declared. "I'll be able to ride them if I get into Cowboy School," she said longingly.

"The place looks deserted," Harry said, looking around. "Where is everyone?"

"At the shindig," Lil said. "We'd better skedaddle!"

Ruby looked at Harry and raised her eyebrows quizzically.

"Everyone's at the audition, so we'd better hurry up," Harry translated. He and Ruby followed Lil round the edge of the corral.

Behind it was a dirt arena packed with small cowboys and cowgirls sitting on piles of hay, watching a young cowboy waving a lasso round his head. It was Hank.

"Yepperdoodles! We're in the nick of time," Lil said.

They watched as Hank let go of the lasso. It flew through the air and looped over a post in the centre of the arena. Everyone cheered. "Whoo-hoo!"

A grown-up cowboy, wearing a string tie and a belt with a bison head on its buckle, came up to the gate where Ruby, Harry, Lil and Puddle were standing.

"Howdy," he said, lifting his hat. "You all here for the audition?"

"Just little old me," Lil said. "I sure would like to be part of your school, Cowboy Clint!"

Hank and Walt ran up, grinning from ear to ear.

"We're both in!" Walt boasted.

"Haven't you quit yet, Lil?" Hank asked. "She's way too small for starting Cowboy School, isn't she, Cowboy Clint?"

"Size isn't important," Cowboy Clint told Lil's brothers. "It's skill that counts." He handed Lil a lasso. "Come on in, Little Lil, and show us what you can do!"

Puddle looked at Lil and wagged his tail.

"Good luck!" Ruby and Harry whispered. They leaned on the gate to watch.

Lil whirled the lasso round her head.

"Yip!" Puddle yapped, and before Ruby could stop him, he squeezed under the gate and raced up to Lil.

"Yip! Yip! Yip!" The naughty little puppy jumped up and tried to grab Lil's lasso.

"Come back, Puddle!" Ruby yelled. "It's not playtime! Lil needs to concentrate..."

But it was too late. Lil glanced down at the puppy scampering around her feet, and her lasso snaked out of control. The swirling rope knocked Cowboy Clint's hat from his head and landed, *plop*, right on top of Puddle.

The hat looked as if it was scampering towards a pile of hay.

"My hat!" Cowboy Clint roared, diving full length after it.

The pile of hay toppled over and buried Puddle, the hat, and Cowboy Clint.

"My audition sure caused a whole heap of trouble," Lil declared, looking at Cowboy Clint's boots sticking out from the hay. His spurs jangled as he kicked his heels.

Ruby and Harry raced over and began to help move the hay.

"Woof!" A little nose appeared under the hay-covered hat. Puddle shook the hat away.

"Woof! Woof!" he barked more loudly.

"Calm down, Puddle," Ruby told him. "You've been naughty enough for one day."

"WOOF! WOOF! WOOF!" Puddle ran to the gate, barking

fit to burst. He was heading in the
direction of the corral.

Ruby, Harry, Lil and all the young
cowboys and cowgirls raced across to
look. A horse rider wearing a spotted
bandana was opening the corral gate.
Ruby's heart skipped a beat. This
time she recognized him. She'd seen
his picture on the WANTED poster!

"It's Outlaw Pete, the horse
rustler!" Ruby yelled. "Stop him!"

But Outlaw Pete was already galloping down the lane, and the horses from the cowboy corral were charging after him.

Cowboy Clint dashed up, pieces of hay stuck all over him.

"That there outlaw rustled all my horses!" he groaned. "And I can't give chase without horses. There's nothing I can do!" He sorrowfully shook his head. Bits of hay sprayed everywhere.

The cowboys and cowgirls looked at each other and shook their heads too. "Nothing we can do," they echoed.

"Well, I can sure do something!" Lil piped up. "I've got a pony and I've got a posse."

"A posse is a group of helpers," Harry whispered to Ruby. "Lil means us!"

"Right," Ruby said. She turned to Cowboy Clint. "We'll get your horses back!"

Chapter Six
Yee Haw!

Ruby, Harry, Lil and Puddle dashed
back to Four Paw Ranch.

"I've got another idea!" Ruby said,
as Lil saddled up Tumbleweed. She
took a couple of empty balloons out
of her pocket.

"Good thinking!" Harry grabbed
a watering can from beside
Tumbleweed's drinking trough and

tipped water into the balloons until they were big and bulgy. He gave one to Ruby.

Lil trotted up on Tumbleweed. Harry leapt up behind her. Ruby scooped Puddle under her arm, and jumped on as well, behind Harry. Lil and Harry were taking up all of Tumbleweed's saddle, so she had to sit on Tumbleweed's warm smooth coat. His tail swished behind her as she grabbed the back of the saddle with her free hand.

"Don't burst my balloon," Ruby warned Puddle as they trotted on to the main street. The little puppy wagged his tail.

Lil glanced over her shoulder. "Which way did Outlaw Pete skedaddle?" she asked.

Harry peered through his dusty glasses. "Out of town," he said, pointing to a trail in the road. "We can follow the tracks."

"Well spotted, Hawkeye Harry," Ruby congratulated him.

Tumbleweed cantered along the trail. The tracks led from Wagging Tail across the cactus plain.

Ruby gripped Tumbleweed tightly with her knees and ducked every time the pony cantered beneath the prickly branches of the tall cacti. It was like being on a fairground ride.

"Look ahead!" Harry pointed to a cloud of dust zigzagging between the cacti. "That's the dust being kicked up by the horses' hooves," he said.

The dust cloud thickened.

"We're getting closer," Ruby breathed. Then, suddenly, the dust cloud began to settle.

"Why are Outlaw Pete and the stolen horses slowing down?" Harry asked.

"The plain is hard for horses to cross," Lil explained. "They're way too big to get under the cacti like Tumbleweed can, so they have to pick their way around them."

"Sometimes it helps to be small,"

85

Ruby said, grinning as she patted Puddle's dusty head.

"Get a move on, Tumbleweed," Lil urged her pony. Tumbleweed's hooves kicked up the dust as he broke into a gallop. Ruby held Puddle and the water balloon tight under one arm, and gripped the back of Tumbleweed's saddle with the other. The hot sun beat down on Ruby's head and the warm desert wind whizzed past her ears as Lil urged Tumbleweed to gallop faster and faster.

Puddle's ears blew back and flapped in the wind. "Yip! Yip! Yip!" he yapped.

"Yee-haw!" Ruby yelled as
Tumbleweed overtook the herd of
stolen horses. "We're catching up
with Outlaw Pete!"

Chapter Seven
Chasing the Outlaw

Soon Tumbleweed was close behind Outlaw Pete's horse.

"Outlaw Pete's having trouble getting through these cacti," Harry commented.

"I'll get him, now!" Lil held on to Tumbleweed's reins with one hand and whirled the lasso around her head with the other. It whizzed through the air. Outlaw Pete pulled back on his horse's reins.

"Ding dang dong, I missed!" Lil coiled the rope for another try.

Outlaw Pete's horse slowed to walking pace as he tried to steer it through a dense clump of prickly cacti.

Ruby and Harry glanced at each other and nodded.

"Showdown time!" Ruby hollered. She and Harry threw their water balloons at Cowboy Pete's back.

Splat! Splat!

Outlaw Pete's back was soaked. Puddle's tail wagged and wagged.

Outlaw Pete looked over his

shoulder. "Hey, stop that!" he yelled. His horse stopped dead in front of a thicket of enormous cacti.

"You should look where you're going!" Harry shouted, as Lil pulled Tumbleweed up beside the outlaw's horse.

Wheeeee! Lil's lasso whizzed through the air and plopped over Outlaw Pete's shoulders, pinning his arms to his sides.

"Three kids and a little doggie aren't getting the better of me," Outlaw Pete growled, leaping down from his horse. The end of the lasso jerked out of Lil's hands.

"Don't let him escape!" Harry shouted, as Outlaw Pete ran towards the thicket of cacti.

There was a loud "WOOF!" as Puddle jumped down from Tumbleweed's back and grabbed the end of the lasso in his teeth.

"Yipper-dee-doo-dah!" Lil yelled, as Puddle ran round and round Outlaw Pete, just as he had run round Hank and Walt. "That's it, truss him up!"

"Well done, Puddle!" Ruby and Harry cheered.

Chapter Eight
Back at the Ranch

Tumbleweed trotted up Wagging
Tail's main street, with Lil, Ruby,
Harry and Puddle on his back.
Lil was leading the trussed-up
Outlaw Pete on the end of her rope.
He stumbled along next to them
in the dust as the stolen horses
walked calmly into town behind
Tumbleweed.

Cowboy Clint and the young cowboys and cowgirls gave a huge cheer when they saw them. Ruby and Harry waved proudly.

The sheriff stepped up, wearing his shiny star badge.

"You did a mighty fine job capturing this real dangerous outlaw!" he declared, as he took the end of the rope from Lil and led Outlaw Pete away to the town jail.

Cowboy Clint beamed. "Little Lil," he said, lifting his hat, "it'd be an honour if you would join my school!" He handed her a little cowboy hat.

Lil took off the one that was too large, and put on the new hat. It was a perfect fit!

Hank came forward with his hat in his hands. "We're mighty sorry for the way we treated you," he told his sister.

"You're a real fine cowgirl, Little Lil," Walt agreed.

"There's no way I could have done it without Rodeo Ruby, Hawkeye Harry and Plum-crazy Puddle!" Lil told the crowd.

"Wahoo!" Everyone cheered as Ruby, Harry and Puddle jumped down from Tumbleweed's back.

Puddle's tail wagged. "Woof!" he barked, and he began to run rings round and round Ruby and Harry, kicking up the dust.

"It's time for us to go home," Ruby called to Lil. "Have fun at Cowboy School!"

"I sure will!" Lil hollered from the back of Tumbleweed as they waved goodbye.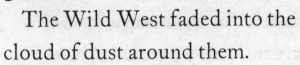

The Wild West faded into the cloud of dust around them.

Back in Grandad's garden, the summer storm had passed and the sun was shining brightly.

"I can't see a thing!" Ruby cried.

"I'm not surprised." Harry laughed.

There was something covering Ruby's eyes. She reached up to push it off. It was a dusty cowboy hat!

"This hat sure is much too big for me!" Ruby declared.

"Maybe you'll grow into it, Rodeo Ruby!" Harry said. "Now, where is that naughty little puppy?"

"Waiting for the next rainy-day adventure," Ruby giggled. "Just like us!"

Can't wait to find out
what Puddle will do next?
Then read on! Here is the first
chapter from Puddle's eleventh
adventure, Holiday Musical . . .

Holiday Musical

Ruby's tin-foil tiara bounced on top of her head as she danced in front of the TV, singing along to her favourite DVD.

"Dance down the hall, you're at Hollywood High, yeah! Life is a ball here at Hollywood..." Ruby ran on the spot in time to the music as it built to the final note. "High!" she yelled and leapt up into the air, her arms stretched wide.

Ruby flopped back on to the settee in Grandad's lounge. She stared at the girl on TV in the sparkly cheerleader outfit. She had dark curly hair and a little dimple in her cheek that you could see whenever she gave her Hollywood smile. "Isn't Charisma Carter amazing, Harry? I could watch that film a hundred times."

Ruby's cousin Harry looked up from the table. He had sticky tape in one hand and a tennis ball in the other.

"You nearly have. I think you're up to ninety-seven," he said, and pushed his glasses into place with the back of his hand.

Harry finished taping the tennis

ball to the end of a cardboard tube, which came from the middle of Grandad's kitchen roll. "There, I've made you a microphone for the red carpet interview with Charisma Carter." Harry held up his new creation.

"And I've got the red carpet," Ruby added. She rolled out a large red bath mat on the floor and stepped on to it.

"You promise that if I pretend to interview you, I can watch *Cosmic Battle Droids* next?" Harry asked.

"I promise," Ruby said. She straightened her tin-foil tiara and tied Grandad's raincoat around her shoulders like an elegant cape.

"Now I'm ready to meet my fans," she said.

Harry pointed the microphone at Ruby. "So . . . um . . . are you excited to be making *Hollywood High Two*?" he asked.

Ruby waved to her imaginary fans. "It's a dream come true." She struck a dramatic pose like the ones she'd seen in all the glossy magazines. "You can take my picture now."

Harry picked up his mobile and used it as a camera.

Ruby could hear the rain drumming against the lounge windows, almost in time to the beat of the music coming from the TV.

Just then, the door to the garden blew open and Puddle, their magical puppy friend, rushed into the room. Puddle always arrived when it rained, and he took them on fantastic adventures.

The little puppy jumped on to the pretend red carpet and shook himself dry.

"Puddle!" Ruby squealed. "We can pretend you're Mrs Whiskers."

"Is that the fluffy white cat with the silly pink tail in *Hollywood High*?" Harry asked.

Ruby nodded and scooped up Puddle. Harry held the tennis ball microphone out to the puppy. Puddle grabbed the tennis ball in his mouth, jumped down and ran straight to the garden.

"Hey, that's our microphone!" Harry called after him. "You naughty puppy."

"I guess it's time for another rainy-day adventure," Ruby said, as she took off her tiara and cape. She giggled. "My fans will have to wait."

The cousins ran out of the door and followed Puddle. He leapt from puddle to puddle down the garden path until he came to just the right one.

Ruby tugged on her plaits for

luck as she, Harry and Puddle
all jumped together and, with
a Hollywood-sized splash,
disappeared.

***

To find out what happens
next, get your copy of
HOLIDAY MUSICAL today!

Magic Mayhem

Ruby and Harry are amazed to find
themselves in a medieval castle...

...when Puddle
takes them on
their latest
adventure! They
meet a magician's
apprentice who is in
deep trouble. He's
lost his spell book.
Can Puddle save
the day?

Find out in MAGIC MAYHEM...

Pirate Surprise

Can you imagine what it's like to
sail on a pirate ship?

Ruby and Harry find
out – when Puddle
takes them on an
amazing adventure
on the high seas!
Captain Redbeard
has a bad case of the
hiccups! Will Puddle
be able to cure him?

Find out in PIRATE SURPRISE…

Animal Antics

Join Puddle, Ruby and Harry
at the Safari Rescue Park!

All the animals
have problems they
need to overcome
before they can be
released into the
wild. Will Puddle
be able to help the
monkey who is
afraid of heights?

Find out in ANIMAL ANTICS...

Puddle
the naughtiest puppy

Christmas
Snow Puppy

Go on a festive adventure with
Ruby, Harry and Puddle!

The children find
themselves in a
beautiful winter
wonderland. Can
they get through
the snow to the
big winter festival
on time?

Find out in CHRISTMAS SNOW PUPPY...

Puddle
the naughtiest puppy

Holiday Musical

It's time for an amazing Hollywood adventure with Ruby, Harry and Puddle!

The children are thrilled when they get to star in a new movie. But the director thinks Puddle has stolen the script! How can Puddle show he's not to blame?

Find out in HOLIDAY MUSICAL…

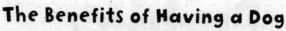

The Benefits of Having a Dog

Hello, it's us again – Ruby, Harry and Puddle! We have just been on a magical journey that was absolutely great. I wonder where we will go next time?

Dogs Trust knows how rewarding it is to have a dog as a pet – so today we are going to talk about all the things that make having a real dog so special for you and your family.

Remember, dogs can be a wonderful part of your family, but it takes a lot of work and time to look after a dog – so if you and your family are thinking of getting a dog, make sure you think it through properly!

Always remember, Puddle is a magical dog, while real dogs and puppies are living animals who need a lot of care, love and attention.

Part of the Family

• Dogs make fantastic companions and are a great addition to your family, as they are so much fun and always want a cuddle.

• A dog can be like your best friend! He or she is always there for you if you are sad or happy. So make sure you spend time with them by playing with them and taking them for lots of walks.

• Going for walks will keep both you and your dog fit, as well as keeping your dog happy!

Can you think of anything else that makes you feel happy? What kind of things do you think your dog might also enjoy?

Congratulations – now you know a little bit more about real dogs, thanks to Dogs Trust! But there is so much more to find out – so join us again in the next story. Take care for now!

Remember, "A dog is for life, not just for Christmas®"
Dogs Trust has 18 Rehoming Centres around the UK and Ireland. To find out more please go to:
 www.dogstrust.org.uk
For more fun and games please go to:
www.learnwithdogs.co.uk

Mystery Circles!

A piece of a character is shown in each circle. Look at the clues and see if you can work out who is shown in each picture.

1. I'm a tiny cowgirl with top lasso skills.

2. We're a pair of Wild West twins.

3. I run the Cowboy School.

4. I'm wanted for livestock rustling.

5. I'm a cute piebald pony.

Cowgirl Shadows!

Lil had a great time meeting Puddle the puppy. Look at the picture of her patting his head, then look at the shadows on the opposite page. Only one of the shadows matches the picture. Can you tell which one it is?

A

B

C

Answers on the next page

Answers to puzzles:
Mystery Circles! 1. Lil, 2. Hank and Walt, 3. Cowboy Clint,
4. Outlaw Pete, 5. Tumbleweed
Cowgirl Shadows! Shadow C

For more magical adventures, come and play with Puddle at

www.puddlethepuppy.com

Use this special code to get extra-special games and free stuff at puddlethepuppy.com

COWBOY HAT